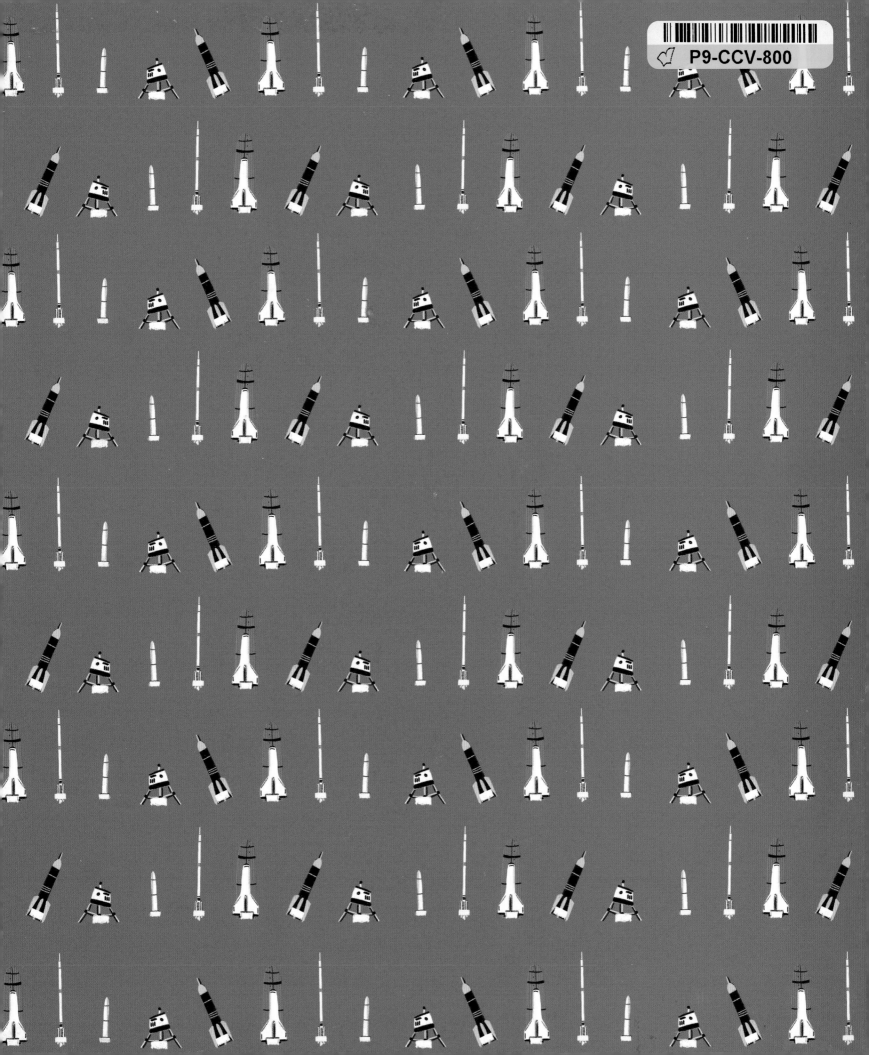

For my very fine friend Ian Salter, a totally cosmic cat. ~ J.C.

To Cian, may your future shine as bright as the stars in the sky. Shine on, dear nephew! ~ A.C.

tiger tales
5 River Road, Suite 128, Wilton, CT 06897
Published in the United States 2019
Originally published in Great Britain 2019
by Caterpillar Books Ltd
Text copyright © 2019 James Carter
Illustrations copyright © 2019 Aaron Cushley
ISBN-13: 978-1-68010-147-8
ISBN-10: 1-68010-147-1
Printed in China
CPB/1400/0971/1018
10 9 8 7 6 5 4 3 2 1

For more insight and activities, visit us at www.tigertalesbooks.com

THE BIG BEYOND

THE STORY OF SPACE TRAVEL

by **James Carter**

Illustrated by **Aaron Cushley**

tiger tales

Once upon a rocket

a countdown has begun

from 10, 9, 8

to 7 and 6

to 5, 4, 3, 2, 1.

Space Shuttle
CHALLENGER

As early people watched the sky,
they wished for wings so they could fly.

They dreamed up questions thick and fast...

How **deep** is **space**?

How **far** are **stars**?

Does planet **Mars** have **life** like ours?

they drew some creatures formed of light:

CRAB

and LION,

BULL

and BEAR.

Such starry beasts
were everywhere.

Through telescopes

we found such things

as planets with their

moons and rings.

We learned we're in the Milky Way,

that stars are all so far away;

the force of space is gravity,

and there are endless galaxies.

GALILEO
GALILEI

Yet still, to fly

was our great aim...

with **kites,**

balloons,

planes.

and gliders,

And then in 1957
rockets soared
toward the heavens.

Through the clouds,
up, UP, and on
out into...

SPUTNIK

THE BIG BEYOND!

UP! we sent beyond the night, to orbit Earth, a satellite.

UP! went creatures—

dogs

and cats,

monkeys, turtles, flies, and rats.

LAIKA

FELIX

UP!

in time went

astronauts,

space explorers,

cosmonauts.

Then summer 1969—

what a time for humankind!

A rocket known as **Saturn Five**

with smoke and flames burst into life.

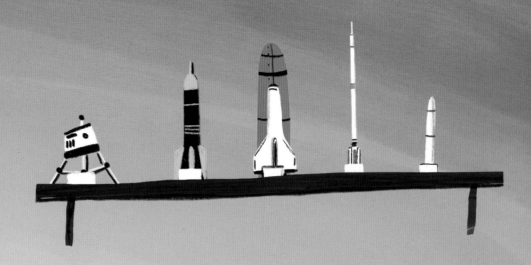

And now, in front of their TVs,

the whole world watched excitedly.

What great adventure happened next?

Upon the **Moon** two men took **steps!**

APOLLO
LUNAR
MODULE

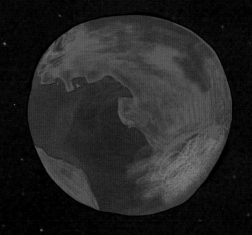

And on that world, so strange and new,

they left a **flag**,

some **footprints**, too.

NEIL ARMSTRONG

BUZZ ALDRIN

Since then we've been
UP many times;
we've walked in space,
launched **satellites**.

And to the planets
spacecraft roam,
sending information
home.

To Mars our neighbor
we've sent more—
probes with which
we could explore;

crafts to land
to test the air,
to sample soil,
to check what's there.

INTERNATIONAL
SPACE
STATION

New **rockets, rockets** every year
will head out through the atmosphere.

We'll need an **astronaut** (or two)—

so what do you think?

Could it be YOU?

LET'S LOOK INTO...

Rockets were invented in China in the 13th century, after the Chinese had discovered how to create gunpowder.

Over the years, rockets have been used as both fireworks and weapons, and since the 1950s, as space-bound craft.

Cosmonaut Yuri Gagarin was the first person to reach space in 1961, in the Russian rocket Vostok 1.

Know how many space travelers there have been so far? More than 500! And at least 200 of these have visited the International Space Station.

Even animals have been sent into space, as humans didn't initially want to risk the dangers. The most well-known is Laika, a Russian stray dog who went into orbit in the spacecraft Sputnik 2 in 1957.

The first astronauts to walk on the Moon were Neil Armstrong and Edwin "Buzz" Aldrin of the American Apollo 11 mission in 1969. Armstrong's words, as he stepped onto the Moon, were, "That's one small step for man, one giant leap for mankind."

Soon there will be tourist trips into space, but you'd better start saving, stargazers—the cost is sky high!